S0-ARY-518

Sheltie™

to the Rescue

Written and illustrated by **Peter Clover**

ALADDIN PAPERBACKS

New York   London   Toronto   Sydney   Singapore

To David Honour

If you purchased this book without a cover, you should be aware
that this book is stolen property. It was reported as "unsold and
destroyed" to the publisher and neither the author nor the publisher
has received any payment for this "stripped book."

First Aladdin Paperbacks edition March 2001
Copyright © 1997 by Working Partners, Limited
First published 1997 by Penguin Books Limited U.K.
Created by Working Partners, Limited

ALADDIN PAPERBACKS
An imprint of Simon & Schuster
Children's Publishing Division
1230 Avenue of the Americas
New York, NY 10020

SHELTIE is a trademark owned
by Working Partners, Limited.
All rights reserved, including the right of
reproduction in whole or in part in any form.
The text for this book was set in Sabon.
Printed and bound in the United States of America
2 4 6 8 10 9 7 5 3 1

Library of Congress Cataloging-in-Publication Data
Clover, Peter.
Sheltie to the rescue / Peter Clover. — 1st Aladdin Paperbacks ed.
p. cm. — (Sheltie ; #5)
Summary: Emma is glad when her parents agree that Sheltie can
come along on the family vacation to the beach and even happier when
he helps to rescue another pony from a dangerous situation.
ISBN 0-689-83976-6
[1. Shetland pony—Fiction. 2. Ponies—Fiction.
3. Vacations—Fiction.] I. Title.

PZ7.C62475 St 2000
[Fic]—dc21
00-062049

Chapter One

"Don't look so grumpy, Emma. It's supposed to be a vacation," said Mom.

They were all sitting around the kitchen table looking at brochures: Mom, Dad, little Joshua, and Emma.

Mom was looking at pictures of pretty seaside cottages. Dad was studying a large road map spread out across the table. And Joshua was trying to turn the pages of the brochure that Mom was holding.

Emma just sat there with her hands folded in her lap, looking grumpy.

"Two whole weeks," said Emma. "It won't be much of a holiday if Sheltie can't come. And who will take care of him while we're away?"

Dad looked up from the map, with a frown.

"We told you yesterday, Emma. Mrs. Linney is going to pop over every day and feed Sheltie. Mrs. Linney knows exactly what to do and how to look after him. There's no need to worry."

"But it won't be the same," said Emma. "Sheltie's *my* pony now. I like looking after him. He'll think I've gone away and left him. He'll be miserable, just like me."

"Two weeks isn't such a long time,"

said Mom. She was beginning to look a little annoyed. "Two weeks at the beach, Emma. Just think of it."

"I don't want to think about it," said Emma. "And I don't want to go. If Sheltie can't come with us then I'd rather stay at home, here in Little Applewood."

Dad raised an eyebrow. He didn't say anything, but Emma could tell he was thinking hard. Mom ignored Emma and kept flipping through the brochures.

"Look at this one. A tiny cottage right on top of the cliffs, overlooking the sea."

Emma glanced at the picture of the little white cottage. But she was too busy thinking about poor Sheltie being left behind with no one to play with for fourteen whole days.

☆ ☆ ☆ ☆

The next morning Emma went into the paddock to give Sheltie his breakfast. She shoveled a scoop of pony mix into Sheltie's feed manger then gave him an extra tiny handful as a treat.

Sheltie stuck his head into the manger and gobbled up the pellets like a vacuum. It always made Emma laugh when Sheltie did that. His head disappeared right inside the bin.

When Sheltie had finished, Emma took the hose from the outside wall and filled his drinking trough.

Sheltie liked the water. He always tried to drink it straight from the hose. Emma aimed the hose at Sheltie and gave him a squirt. Sheltie blew a loud raspberry, then galloped playfully around the paddock.

When Emma looked up, she saw Mom and Dad standing by the paddock gate. They were both smiling. Joshua was there too, sitting across the top bar of the wooden fence. He was squirming like a little worm and Mom was holding on to him tightly.

Emma put the hose away and skipped over to the gate. She was ready for her own breakfast now, and as they all sat around the kitchen table, Mom told Emma some special news.

"Do you remember the cottage we were looking at yesterday, Emma?" said Mom. "The one on the cliff, overlooking the sea?"

Emma nodded and looked down at her shoes. She didn't want to think about going away on vacation and leaving Sheltie.

"Well, Emma," said Dad, "the cottage has a paddock at the back just like Sheltie's."

"But Sheltie won't be in it, will he?" said Emma in a sulky voice. "Poor Sheltie will be left behind all on his own!"

Dad raised an eyebrow at Mom then looked at Emma and smiled.

"Oh, no he won't," said Dad. "I called Mrs. Linney this morning and she has a friend who is going to lend us a horse trailer. So now Sheltie can come away on vacation too."

Emma's face lit up with a big smile and she clapped her hands with excitement.

"Do you really mean it, Dad? Yippee! Now it will be a real vacation for all of us."

Chapter Two

Two days before the vacation, Dad picked up the horse trailer. It looked like a little caravan on wheels. There was a big door at the back and a little window high up at the front for Sheltie to look out and see where he was going. The horse trailer was just the right size to take a little Shetland pony like Sheltie.

"It's just like a little house," said Emma as she peered inside.

When Emma ran to the paddock and told Sheltie that he was coming on vacation, he became quite frisky and galloped around the little field tossing his head. She knew he was as excited as she was.

The next morning Emma was busy helping Mom and Dad pack their suitcases with everything they would need for two weeks at the seashore.

Then in the afternoon Emma helped Dad load Sheltie's bags of pony mix and several bales of hay into the horse trailer. She hung Sheltie's bridle and saddle on the special hooks behind the door, then spread some straw across the floor.

Everything was ready for an early start the following day.

Bright and early on Friday morning Dad

tied the suitcases to the roof rack on top of the car. Emma put Sheltie's head collar on him and led him up the ramp into the horse trailer.

Sheltie gave a soft blow and looked out of the little window. His bright eyes twinkled with excitement beneath his bushy mane.

Sheltie had never been away on vacation before, and Emma was looking forward to galloping along the sandy beach and wading with him in the sea.

Little Joshua was excited, too, and held on tightly to his bucket and spade.

It was ten o'clock when they finally set off for Summerland Bay. Sheltie's horse trailer trundled along smoothly behind the car. Emma sat in the backseat next to the window. Mom sat in the back, too, with

Joshua strapped into his special car seat.

As they drove along, Emma kept looking behind to make sure the horse trailer was still there. Sometimes Emma could see the tip of Sheltie's nose poking through the trailer window. It was open slightly and

Sheltie was sniffing the air. She knew he was enjoying every minute of the ride.

The trip took two hours, so it was midday when they finally arrived at their cottage.

Cliff-top Cottage was much smaller than the house in Little Applewood. It was whitewashed, with a bright red door. On either side of the door were two little windows. Upstairs there were two bedrooms and a bathroom.

At the back of the cottage was a small paddock for Sheltie. The cottage itself sat high on the cliff top, with fields and meadows all around. The rolling heath ran to the edge of the cliff. And below, a footpath wound its way gently down to the sandy beach of Summerland Bay. It was a beautiful spot. The perfect place for a vacation.

Chapter Three

Before they unloaded their suitcases from the roof rack, Dad helped Emma settle Sheltie into his paddock.

Sheltie's nostrils twitched as he took in a deep breath of salty air. Sheltie had never smelled the sea before. It made him feel lively, and he galloped around his new paddock in a full circle, shaking his long mane and kicking his heels. Sheltie seemed very happy. And Emma was delighted too.

Dad took the suitcases and carried them into the cottage. Then Emma helped Mom unpack all their things.

Dad made some sandwiches and a pot of tea, and everyone sat down outside at a little table in the garden. Emma and Joshua had sodas and looked out across the cliff top at the sparkling sea beyond.

After lunch they all went for a walk to explore the footpath that led down to the beach.

Sheltie didn't go. He was busy in his new paddock making friends with three stray ducks. Sheltie had rounded up the ducks into a tight corner and stood with his head on one side listening to their noisy quacking.

Dad gave Joshua a piggyback ride as

they all made their way slowly down the footpath to the beach.

At the end of the footpath there were twenty-eight wooden steps which led down on to the sand. Emma counted them all.

Once on the beach, Emma ran down toward the sea. She pulled off her shoes and socks and waded in the foamy waves.

Farther down along the beach some people were sitting on the sand: a man and a woman, and a young girl about Emma's age with dark, curly hair. When the girl saw Emma, she got up and walked down to the sea.

Emma made a face. The girl was Alice Parker. She went to the same school as Emma. Emma didn't like Alice Parker very much. She was a show-off and was always teasing Emma about Sheltie. Alice Parker had a pony too. Not a little Shetland Pony like Sheltie, but a big brown one that shone like copper.

Alice Parker was always saying that Sheltie had funny, stumpy legs and wasn't a real pony at all. And she said that Emma looked stupid when she was riding him.

The two girls met at the water's edge.

"Hello, Alice," said Emma, trying to be friendly.

Alice stuck her nose up in the air.

"Are you on vacation too?" asked Emma.

Alice didn't answer. She just turned and walked away.

Emma plodded back up the beach toward Mom, Dad, and Joshua.

"Guess who's over there," said Emma to Mom. She pointed along the beach with her finger.

"Is it someone you know?" asked Dad.

"It's Alice Parker from school," said Emma. "She's horrible."

Mom looked over at Alice, who was now picking shells up from the sand.

"She looks like a nice girl, Emma. Why don't you give her a chance? After all, if she's here on vacation too, it might be nice to have someone to play with."

"Not Alice Parker," said Emma. "Besides, I've already tried." She made a face. "I'd much rather play with Joshua and Sheltie. Alice Parker calls Sheltie names. I'll never like her."

"Maybe you'll change your mind in a day or two, Emma," said Dad.

"I won't," said Emma, feeling very determined. She didn't like Alice Parker at school, and she wasn't going to like her on vacation. And that was that.

Chapter Four

The next day Emma took Sheltie down to the beach. Sheltie was a tough little pony with a strong, steady walk. It was easy for him to take the winding footpath down to the sandy bay. But he couldn't manage the twenty-eight wooden steps, so everyone went the long way down.

Dad walked in front with Joshua sitting on his shoulders. Mom followed, carrying a picnic basket and towels for all of them to sit on.

Emma led Sheltie by his reins. Sheltie plodded along, enjoying every minute of the sea breeze as it blew through his long shaggy mane. Overhead, the cries of the seagulls echoed in the blue sky. It was a beautiful summer's day.

Down on the sandy beach Emma climbed into Sheltie's saddle.

"Let's go, Sheltie." Emma pressed with her heels, and Sheltie trotted off across the bay, leaving a trail of little hoofprints in the soft golden sand.

At the water's edge, Sheltie stopped. He had never seen the sea before, and he gazed out across the sparkling water. A crab scuttled by at his feet. Sheltie gave a loud blow and tossed his head as he pawed at the lapping waves.

Mom had laid the towels out on the sand, and Joshua plonked himself down with his bucket and shovel. Dad watched Emma and Sheltie trotting along in the surf.

"Don't go too far, Emma. Stay where we can see you," called Dad.

Emma smiled back over her shoulder. "We will," she said. She rode Sheltie down to the end of the bay. Giant rocks sloped down from the cliffs into the sea. And there Summerland Bay came to an end.

There were little rock pools at the end of the beach. Emma dismounted to take a better look. Sheltie peered into a pool and saw his reflection in the water. Then he stuck his nose in and pulled out a long slimy string of seaweed. Sheltie gave the seaweed a good shake, and Emma got sprayed with droplets of salt water.

Emma grabbed the other end of the seaweed. Sheltie held on fast and pulled. The seaweed tore apart and Emma sat down on the sand with a bump.

Sheltie pranced around with the seaweed hanging from his mouth. He looked very funny—like a pony with a long, green beard.

Emma laughed as she stood up and brushed the sand from her jeans. Just then she noticed another pony and a rider coming along the beach, close to the water's edge. It was Alice Parker.

"Oh, no!" said Emma.

Alice Parker was riding a handsome white pony. Not a little Shetland pony like Sheltie, but a much bigger one.

Alice saw Emma and came trotting over. She brought the pony to a halt and gave a smug smile.

"Hello, Emma," said Alice. "I see you've brought Stumpy on vacation with you."

"His name's Sheltie," said Emma. She was really mad. Emma found it hard to like Alice.

"This is Silver Lad," said Alice. "We're

staying at Highcliff Farm. They have lots of ponies there. Real ponies. It's a riding center. I bet you wish you had a real pony to ride, don't you, Emma?"

"No, I don't. I only like Sheltie. And anyway, he *is* a real pony. He's a Shetland pony."

Sheltie walked over to Silver Lad and looked up at the white pony. Their noses met and they sniffed each other and said hello.

"I'll race you," said Alice, smirking. "Silver Lad against Stumpy."

"I don't want to race," frowned Emma. She climbed back up into Sheltie's saddle.

"You're scared," said Alice. "I bet Stumpy can't even run. His legs are too short!"

"Yes he can," snapped Emma. "Sheltie's really fast."

"Come on then, scaredy-cat," laughed Alice. "Race you to the other end of the beach!"

Then Alice dug in her heels and Silver Lad took off at a canter along the stretch of beach.

Emma didn't really want to race. But Sheltie did.

Emma just squeezed gently with her

heels, and he was away in a flash. Sheltie galloped after Silver Lad as fast as his little legs could carry him.

Emma hung on tightly to the reins as Sheltie raced along the shore. He wasn't fast enough though, and Silver Lad won the race easily.

"I told you," laughed Alice Parker. "I told you that Stumpy couldn't run."

Emma said nothing. She was upset and angry. It wasn't fair. Sheltie only had little legs. Emma turned Sheltie around and walked him back along the beach.

She leaned forward and patted Sheltie's neck.

"Never mind, boy. You're better than Silver Lad any day!"

Chapter Five

The next morning Emma didn't want to go down to the beach. She didn't want to meet Alice Parker again.

Instead, she asked Mom if she could ride Sheltie out over the meadow. There was a bridle path that led off from their cottage across the grass.

Mom said it was okay as long as Emma kept away from the cliff top and didn't go too far. Emma promised, then she and

Sheltie set off on an adventure all their own.

Emma rode Sheltie along the bridle path. It was nice and quiet up there. Sheep were grazing peacefully all across the meadow. The best thing of all, though, was that there was no Alice Parker.

Emma had been riding for about ten minutes when she noticed something glinting up ahead, just off the bridle path.

What's that funny-looking thing? thought Emma. It was a metal bar gleaming between the bushes. Emma dismounted and walked up to it.

The shiny bar turned out to be the handle of a silver shopping cart. Just like the ones they have in supermarkets.

What's that doing up here in the middle of nowhere? Emma thought.

Sheltie saw it too and trotted over to investigate. There were some white things sticking out between the bars of the cart. They were feathers. Three long, white feathers. Emma pulled them free and Sheltie tried to eat them.

"I wonder what kind of bird these came from?" Emma said to Sheltie. Sheltie put his head over to one side, listening carefully.

The feathers were very long.

"It must have been a big bird," said Emma. "A seagull perhaps!" She looked up at the sky. Sheltie looked up too. But the feathers seemed far too long for a seagull.

"Maybe it was an ostrich," laughed Emma. She held the feathers together at one end like a fan and climbed back into the saddle.

They continued on their way across the meadow. Emma pretended that she was a lost princess riding across the desert. She waved the fan and tickled Sheltie's ears. Sheltie swished his tail and blew a loud raspberry.

Half an hour later, when Emma and Sheltie came back along the bridle path, the supermarket cart was gone.

How strange! thought Emma. Who on earth would have pushed a cart all the way up to the meadow and then taken it away again? Emma was puzzled by the mystery.

They continued slowly back to the cottage, following the path around the curve of a hill.

Suddenly the narrow track dipped sharply and Sheltie stumbled. When Sheltie started to walk again, he was limping.

"Oh, poor Sheltie," said Emma. She slid out of the saddle. "Have you hurt your leg?" Sheltie lowered his head and stood holding his front hoof up off the ground. Emma felt his leg and looked at his hoof, but she couldn't see anything. She was really worried.

"You poor thing. Can you manage the rest of the way? It's not far now."

Sheltie hobbled forward, limping, as Emma led with the reins. They walked very slowly. Each time Sheltie's foot touched the ground he lifted it again very quickly.

Emma led Sheltie off the hard stony track and on to the soft grass. She hoped it was nothing serious. She wanted to get Sheltie back to the cottage as quickly as possible.

"If we cut across here, it won't be so far," said Emma. They walked away from the winding bridle path. Sheltie limped on as best as he could.

Suddenly the grass ahead sloped away down into a big dip, like a giant basin in the landscape. They stood on its rim overlooking the roof of an old tumbledown cottage.

Maybe someone there could help, thought Emma.

Chapter Six

A little path wound its way down to the front door. Dandelions grew up all over the front step. It looked as though nobody lived in the cottage after all.

Then Emma saw the supermarket cart parked outside and her eyes grew wide.

While Emma was staring, an old woman came out of the cottage. She held a ginger cat cradled in her arms like a baby.

"Hello," called the old woman. She was

dressed in a funny old raincoat tied at the waist with string. But she had a nice, friendly smile.

"Hello," said Emma.

"Have you come to see the animals?" asked the old woman.

Emma didn't know what to say.

"We're staying at Cliff-top Cottage," she said. "We're on vacation. This is Sheltie. He's hurt his leg and he's limping."

Sheltie shook his mane and whinnied softly. He stood with his head low, looking at his hoof.

"Better bring him down and let me have a look at him," said the old woman. Her voice sounded kind and caring.

Emma led Sheltie down the winding path into the little front yard. The old woman put the cat down and came over. She felt Sheltie's leg, then lifted his hoof and had a good look at it.

"He's got a stone caught under his shoe," said the old woman. "I'll fix that. Your little pony will soon be as good as new."

She went into the cottage and came out holding a hoof pick. Sheltie stood very still and let the old woman lift his leg. She then carefully removed the stone from his hoof.

"There, that's better, isn't it, Sheltie?"

Sheltie could put his foot down comfortably now.

"What a nice, friendly pony." The woman gave Sheltie a hard pat.

Emma liked the old woman. Her name was Mary. She looked funny, but she was very kind.

Mary lived in the cottage by herself and cared for all kinds of sick and injured animals. People brought them to the cottage for Mary to look after. And sometimes the animals came all by themselves.

Mary asked Emma if she would like to see the animals. Emma said she would, but she thought she'd better ask Mom and Dad first.

It wasn't far to Cliff-top Cottage. Luckily Sheltie's hoof was as good as new, and he trotted back happily along the bridle path.

In no time at all Mom and Dad got to hear all about Mary and how she had helped Sheltie. Emma also told them about Mary's animal hospital and asked if she could go back and see all the animals. Dad said he would go with her that afternoon.

After lunch Emma plopped the saddle on to Sheltie's back and tightened the leather girth around his fat tummy. Then she slipped on the bridle and mounted.

Mom and Joshua stood outside the cottage and watched as Emma, Sheltie, and Dad made their way along the bridle path and out over the meadow.

"Bye-bye," gurgled Joshua, who was just learning to talk.

"Be back at six in time for dinner, you two!" Mom called after them. Emma smiled and waved. Sheltie blew a raspberry and made Dad laugh.

Mary came out of the cottage when she heard Emma, Sheltie, and Dad approaching.

"Hello," Dad called cheerfully when he saw Mary.

Mary greeted them with a warm smile. "Hello, Emma. Hello, Sheltie."

Sheltie shook his head and tossed his mane.

Dad introduced himself, then Mary took them behind the cottage to see the animal hospital and to meet all her patients.

There was Harold, a hairy goat with a lame leg, and Doris, an old seaside donkey that nobody wanted anymore. Poor Doris was blind in one eye. Harold and Doris both lived in a little field in back of the cottage.

A fox that had been hit by a car lay on some straw in a wire cage.

"He's still healing," said Mary. "But he's going to be fine."

There was a badger, too, that had hurt its foot, several rabbits, a family of hedgehogs, two seagulls, and an owl.

And in a wooden pen at the far end of Mary's hospital was a beautiful white swan.

"This is Snowy," said Mary. "He flew into some overhead wires and damaged his wing. It's mended now, but he won't be able to fly for a while. Every day I put Snowy in the shopping cart and take him up to Hollow's Pond in the meadow. He has a little swim and then I bring him back. He's very gentle. When he can fly and take care of himself, I'll release him back into the wild."

Now Emma knew where those long white feathers came from!

Mary told Emma and Dad how all the animals would eventually go back to their homes when they were well enough. All except Harold and Doris. They were like family to Mary.

"If you like, Emma," said Mary, "tomorrow you can come with me to Hollow's Pond and watch Snowy swim. Would that be all right?"

"Oh, can I please, Dad?" said Emma.

Dad said she could. He liked Mary and thought she was a kind person.

"And can Sheltie come too?" asked Emma.

"Of course," said Mary.

Sheltie threw back his head and let out the loudest snort Emma had ever heard. Sheltie liked Mary too.

Chapter Seven

In the morning Mom gave Emma two small fruit pies which she had brought from home. She popped them into a paper bag for Emma to take along to Mary.

Dad went with Emma and Sheltie as far as Mary's cottage, just to make sure that the visit to Hollow's Pond was still all right.

Mary was out in the back field, hand-feeding Harold the goat and Doris the donkey with carrots and apple quarters.

Emma rode Sheltie around to the back of the cottage and right up to the fence.

Harold stood on his hind legs with his front hooves resting on the wooden rail and rubbed noses with Sheltie. Doris gave a low bray, her way of saying, "Hello, Sheltie."

Emma slipped out of the saddle and held Sheltie's reins. She smiled at Dad and handed Mary the fruit pies.

"What a lovely treat," said Mary. "I know who would like a piece of these." Harold was doing a funny little dance and staring at the paper bag.

"You can have a piece later, you greedy goat," laughed Mary.

She took the pies inside, then went to Snowy's pen and gently put the swan in the shopping cart. Snowy seemed very tame and didn't mind Mary picking him up. Emma guessed that Snowy was looking forward to his morning swim.

Mary pushed the cart and Dad watched Emma lead Sheltie up the narrow track that led the way from the cottage.

"See you back at home," said Dad.

Hollow's Pond wasn't very far. It was

near the spot where Emma had first seen the shopping cart hidden in the bushes.

Mary lifted Snowy from the cart and carried him over a grassy hump and down into a shallow dip on the other side. In the hollow was a little secret pond, hidden away from the rest of the meadow. You would never have guessed that there was a pond there at all if you didn't know about it.

Long reeds grew all around the pond at the water's edge. Mary lowered Snowy to the ground, and the swan waddled into the shallow water. He waggled his tail feathers and swam out to the middle of the pond.

Emma and Sheltie watched as Snowy glided gracefully across the water. He looked so beautiful. No one would ever have known that he had damaged his wing.

Sheltie grazed on the grassy bank, nibbling at a patch of dandelions, while Emma and Mary watched the swan.

After a while, Mary took some lettuce leaves from her pocket and dipped them in the water. Snowy glided over and waddled up on to the bank. He took the leaves and then shook his tail feathers. Mary picked him up and carried him back to the cart.

"Before we go back," said Mary, "I'll show you another secret."

"Another secret!" chirped Emma.

Sheltie pricked up his ears.

Mary told Emma about a pair of peregrine falcons which were nesting on a ledge on the cliff face.

"They are very rare birds," Mary said. "And they're hatching eggs. Come on!"

Chapter Eight

They pushed the cart across to the cliff top.

Emma tethered Sheltie and followed Mary to the edge of the cliff.

Mary held Emma's hand and they stood looking down the steep cliff face.

"Be careful now, Emma," said Mary. "Don't stand too near."

They peered over the edge. Below, halfway down, a narrow path hugged the cliff face. And beyond that, a long, long way down, was the beach. Emma could see Alice Parker down there riding Silver Lad along the shore.

Emma noticed how far down the beach was. Her legs felt wobbly. Alice Parker looked *so* tiny, like a small, round pebble.

Mary pointed to a ledge. Two falcons were perched on the rocky lip. One bird was sitting on a nest.

"The eggs should hatch soon," said Mary. "And we should see two fluffy chicks before the week is out."

"Oh," cooed Emma. "That'd be great."

Then Emma looked at the cliff path.

"Where does that lead to?" she asked.

"The cliff path runs right down to the beach," said Mary. "But it's very dangerous. Don't *you* ever go down there," she added.

"I won't," said Emma. The path looked far too dangerous. Although there were some wider areas, it was mostly very narrow.

Emma was back at Cliff-top Cottage in time for lunch. Dad had made some sandwiches, and they all sat outside in the yard to eat them. Then they had some delicious strawberry ice cream.

Emma was so excited. She told Mom and Dad all about Snowy and how graceful he was when he swam. And she told them about the peregrine falcons and the nest.

"You were very lucky to see a pair nesting like that," said Dad. "You must be careful not to disturb them."

Emma smiled. "Don't worry, they're too far away." She was having such a wonderful vacation.

That afternoon they left Sheltie in the paddock, grazing in the summer sunshine, and went for a drive to the little quay around the next bay.

Colorful fishing boats bobbed up and down in the harbor. Emma's family walked along the beach collecting shells. Emma found a piece of driftwood in the shape of a fish. Mom said she would help Emma paint it. Emma wanted to give the driftwood to Mary as a present when they left.

Mom said she would like to meet Mary and visit her animal hospital. She wanted Joshua to see Snowy and the animals. And Dad was hoping to see the two falcons.

When they arrived back at Cliff-top Cottage, Emma decided to ride Sheltie across the meadow. She said she would ask Mary if it would be all right to bring the whole family over the following day.

Mary's cottage was only a ten minute ride away, but when Emma and Sheltie got there, Mary was nowhere to be seen. All the animals were there. Harold and Doris were in the field. The cart was there, and

Snowy was in his little pen. But there was
no sign of Mary.

Emma thought that maybe Mary had
gone to watch the falcons. She turned
Sheltie and rode over to the cliff top. Mary
wasn't there either.

Emma stood up in the stirrups and looked around. She couldn't see Mary anywhere.

Sheltie raised his head and sniffed at the air. Then he blew a loud snort.

Emma slid off the saddle and left Sheltie to nibble at the grass as he usually did. But Sheltie was more interested in the edge of the cliff top. He trotted over to the rocky edge and gave several more noisy snorts. Then Sheltie pawed at the rock with his hoof.

What is he so upset about? thought Emma. She went over to take a look. Emma stood as near to the edge of the cliff as she dared and peered over. She gasped in horror at what she saw.

There below, on the narrow cliff path, were Alice Parker and Silver Lad!

Chapter Nine

Emma could see that Alice had taken Silver Lad up the cliff path from the beach and now they were stuck. The poor pony was terrified and had refused to go any farther.

Alice stood beside Silver Lad on the narrow path, unable to move. She looked very scared.

It was a long way down to the beach and the cliff face was very steep. Alice clung on to Silver Lad's reins and looked up at Emma, pressing herself against the cliff wall. She was so happy to see Emma that she burst into tears.

"Please help!" sobbed Alice. "We're stuck. Silver Lad won't move. He won't go forward and I'm scared to turn him." Alice was really very frightened. Her face was almost white.

"Just stay there and keep still," said Emma. "Don't move at all. I'll take Sheltie and get help."

Emma thought she would ride back to Mary's cottage to see if she had come home. But then she thought she could gallop back quickly and fetch Dad. He'd know what to do.

But before Emma could do anything, Sheltie had gone to the rescue. He had seen where the cliff path began between a gap in the two big rocks and was already on his way.

"Sheltie!" called Emma. "Come back!"

But it seemed as though Sheltie knew that Alice and Silver Lad were in serious trouble. He carefully stepped onto the narrow path.

It was very steep at first, but then the path leveled out a bit and became a little wider.

Emma followed behind Sheltie. She was scared but took the path slowly, one step at a time.

"Be careful," cried Alice from below.

Silver Lad let out a pitiful whinny.

Sheltie was a very brave pony. And being small, with a strong steady walk, he was able to tread the path easily. Emma walked close behind, keeping her back to

the cliff wall and moving along sideways,
trying not to look down.

The wind whipped her cheeks and the
waves crashed onto the beach below. Emma
bit her bottom lip and called to Alice.

"We're coming! Don't be scared," Emma
shouted, even though she was scared herself.

Sheltie carried on. He was very surefooted and didn't seem to be afraid. He seemed determined to rescue Alice and Silver Lad.

As he moved forward, Emma drew in her breath and stood watching, as still as a statue. She could see that the pathway just in front of Sheltie was dangerously narrow. And one small part was missing where the rock had crumbled away.

Emma gasped as Sheltie nearly put his foot over the edge.

"Sheltie, please be careful," cried Emma.

Sheltie looked around and shook his head with a loud snort as if to say, "I'm all right, Emma."

Chapter Ten

With only a few feet left to go, Sheltie suddenly heard a voice calling from above. He looked up. It was Mary. She looked very worried as she peered down at Emma and Sheltie from the cliff top above them.

"Be careful, Emma," called Mary. "Don't make any sudden movements, and stay close to the cliff face. I'm coming to get you."

Mary began to climb down onto the

path. Emma edged her way back and took Mary's outstretched hand.

From the cliff top they could see that Sheltie had reached Alice. He stood on a wider piece of path just in front of Silver Lad and turned around.

Emma called down to Alice. "Reach forward and grab Sheltie's tail!"

Alice was so frightened she could hardly move. Sheltie gave a soft snort.

Mary spoke softly to Alice. "Move forward slowly," she said. "Look straight ahead. Hold on tightly to Sheltie's tail and lead the other pony."

Alice took Silver Lad's reins. Then, holding on to Sheltie's tail, they all began to move slowly.

Seeing Sheltie seemed to give Silver Lad

the courage he needed to move forward. The frightened pony trod carefully and followed Alice and Sheltie.

When Sheltie reached the narrowest part where the path had crumbled away, Emma called down gently to Sheltie. "Go on, boy. Just a little farther."

Sheltie looked up and answered with a soft blow. He carefully stepped past the crumbling edge and led Alice on. But Silver Lad was too frightened. The pony stopped again and Alice had to let go of his rein.

Mary went down onto the path again and called Sheltie forward. She reached out for his rein and helped him along the last bit, up onto the cliff top.

When they were safely away from the path, Alice burst into tears.

"I was so scared," she sobbed, and threw her arms around Emma, giving her a big hug.

Before anyone had time to blink, Sheltie went back down onto the path. Silver Lad was still stuck. The poor pony was terrified and all on his own.

Sheltie stood at the start of the path and

made funny pony noises: soft snorts and whinnies that called to Silver Lad as if to say, "Come on, you're nearly there."

Sheltie nodded his head and Silver Lad moved slowly forward on his own. He trod with care and began walking toward Sheltie.

Mary, Emma, and Alice held their breath as Sheltie and Silver Lad clambered up onto the cliff top.

Sheltie nuzzled up to Silver Lad. The poor pony was shaking from head to hoof.

Mary stroked the pony's muzzle and spoke softly to him. Her voice soon calmed Silver Lad down.

Emma went over to Sheltie and put her arms around his neck.

"Oh, Sheltie. You were so brave."

Sheltie gave a loud snort, then pushed

his soft velvet muzzle against Emma's cheek and blew hot air down the side of her neck.

"You have a very special pony, Emma," said Alice.

"I know," said Emma. "I don't know what would have happened if it wasn't for Sheltie."

Alice had stopped crying. "I'm sorry I've been so horrible to you and Sheltie, Emma." Her eyes were all red and puffy. She looked very embarrassed. "I can't thank you and Sheltie enough for saving us." Alice looked down at her shoes.

"We had better get you two back home," said Mary.

They led the two ponies back to Mary's cottage, and the old woman telephoned Highcliff Farm, where Alice was staying.

Alice's mother and father drove up with a man from the riding school to collect Alice and Silver Lad. They were both very grateful to Emma and said they would like to send her a little present as a special thank-you when they got back to Little Applewood.

Emma rode back to Cliff-top Cottage on Sheltie to tell Mom and Dad all about their adventure.

"What a silly thing to do," said Mom. "Taking a pony up such a dangerous path."

Although Mom and Dad said that Emma should never have attempted to rescue Alice alone, they understood that Sheltie had taken the lead. Emma and Sheltie had been very brave. Mom and Dad were so proud of their daughter and her little pony.

"It's a good thing Sheltie came along with us on vacation after all, isn't it, Mom?" said Emma.

Chapter Eleven

The rest of the vacation passed by very quickly. Emma didn't see Alice Parker on the beach again. Not even once. Apart from a few other families they had the golden sands all to themselves.

Each day Emma rode Sheltie along the shore. Sheltie was excited by the smell of the sea and the soft ground beneath his feet. He pranced about on the sand and Emma raced him along the stretch of the beach, sending the seagulls screaming and soaring over their heads. It was wonderful.

Every day they also went to visit Mary and the animals.

By the following week the fox was up and walking, and Mary said that in another week he would be strong enough to be released back into the wild.

The badger was getting better too. And Snowy could now spread his wings and flap them with ease. He still couldn't fly yet, but Mary said that he soon would.

Emma and Sheltie also went with Mary to Hollow's Pond and watched the swan take his daily swim.

"Just think," said Emma, "when I'm back home, Snowy's wing will be as good as new, and he'll be flying free. Do you think he will remember us?"

"I'm sure he will," smiled Mary. "How could anyone forget you and Sheltie?"

Sheltie blew a raspberry and shook his mane.

They strolled to the edge of the cliff top and watched the two falcons. The mother falcon sat on the nest, and Mary said that the eggs should be hatching very soon.

On their last full day in Summerland Bay, Emma and Sheltie took Mom, Dad, and Joshua to visit Mary. They saw all the animals and strolled up to the cliff top to see the falcons.

The two chicks had finally hatched! They sat in the nest and poked their fluffy little heads out from beneath their mother's wing.

Dad looked through his binoculars as the male falcon brought food to the nest.

"Birdy!" Joshua laughed.

"This has been the best vacation ever," said Emma.

Before they left, Emma gave Mary the painted driftwood fish that Mom had helped her to decorate as a present. It was beautifully painted, with colorful scales, eyes, and fins.

"I will treasure it always," said Mary with a little tear in the corner of her eye. She gave Emma a big hug.

Sheltie nuzzled Mary's cheek with his nose and gave her face a lick.

Chapter Twelve

The next morning the holiday finally came to an end.

Emma helped Mom pack up all their things, and Dad tied the suitcases on the roof rack on top of the car.

When everything was ready, Emma felt very sad to leave the cottage. Sheltie was settled safely in the horse trailer, and they climbed into the car and set off for home.

Mary had come to the cottage to say

good-bye, and Emma and Joshua waved as the car pulled away and disappeared down the driveway and out onto the main road.

"I'll write to you from Little Applewood," Emma called through the open window.

Mary smiled and waved until the car was out of sight.

At home Emma told her best friend Sally all about her wonderful vacation. Sally had ridden over on Minnow as soon as she knew they were back. Sheltie liked Minnow, and his eyes twinkled with delight when he saw him.

Emma and Sally went riding together all over the countryside around Little Applewood. And when they rode up to Horseshoe Pond, they sat and talked about Mary, Snowy the swan, and all the animals in Mary's hospital.

Emma wrote to Mary, and very soon afterward a letter arrived for Emma from Summerland Bay. Inside the envelope along with Mary's reply was a cutting from the local newspaper. DARING CLIFF-TOP RESCUE was the heading on the page.

Mom read the article aloud:

"While on vacation at Summerland Bay, brave Emma Matthews and her fearless Shetland pony, Sheltie, came to the rescue of Alice Parker and her pony Silver Lad when they became trapped on the cliff path overlooking the sea. Without a thought for his own safety, brave Sheltie climbed down onto the narrow cliff path and with Emma's help led the trapped girl and her pony to safety in a daring rescue. Emma Matthews and Sheltie live in Little Applewood."

"You and Sheltie are famous, Emma!" said Dad.

Emma blushed with pride. She was very pleased. "But it was Sheltie really," said Emma.

That morning a package had also arrived for Emma. It was from Mr. and Mrs. Parker. Emma ripped open the wrapping paper and inside was a lovely little book all about Shetland ponies. There was also a note from Alice. It read:

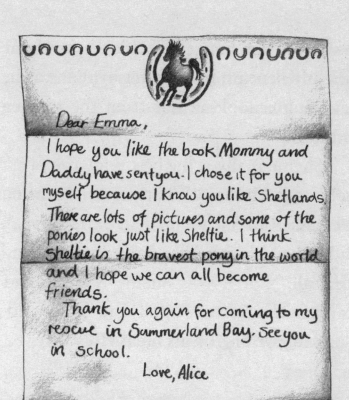

Dear Emma,

I hope you like the book Mommy and Daddy have sent you. I chose it for you myself because I know you like Shetlands. There are lots of pictures and some of the ponies look just like Sheltie. I think Sheltie is the bravest pony in the world and I hope we can all become friends.

Thank you again for coming to my rescue in Summerland Bay. See you in school.

Love, Alice

"What a nice letter," said Mom.

Outside, Sheltie was waiting in the paddock for his breakfast. He was tossing his head and making the noises he always did when he was hungry. Sheltie's eyes shone brightly beneath his long bushy mane as he saw Emma looking out from the kitchen window.

"Sheltie really is the best pony ever, isn't he?" said Emma. "What a great vacation we had. And Sheltie made it extra special, didn't he? Maybe Alice Parker isn't so bad after all."

Then she trotted happily out to the paddock to give Sheltie his breakfast.